ISLA to ISLAND

ISLA to ISLAND

ALEXIS CASTELLANOS

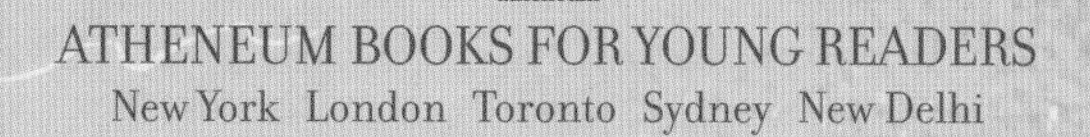

ATHENEUM BOOKS FOR YOUNG READERS
New York London Toronto Sydney New Delhi

Mom, Talco, y Bella

This is my contribution since I never developed the taste for oysters.

atheneum

ATHENEUM BOOKS FOR YOUNG READERS
An imprint of Simon & Schuster Children's Publishing Division
1230 Avenue of the Americas, New York, New York 10020

Also available in an Atheneum Books for Young Readers paperback edition

Interior design by Karyn Lee
The text for this book was hand-lettered.
The illustrations for this book were rendered digitally.
Manufactured in China
1221 SCP

First Atheneum Books for Young Readers hardcover edition March 2022 • 2 4 6 8 10 9 7 5 3 1 • Library of Congress Cataloging-in-Publication Data • Names: Castellanos, Alexis, author, illustrator. • Title: Isla to island / Alexis Castellanos. • Description: New York : Atheneum Books for Young Readers, 2022. | Audience: Ages 10 up | Audience: Grades 7–9 | Summary: "A wordless graphic novel in which twelve-year-old Marisol must adapt to a new life 1960s Brooklyn after her parents send her to the United States from Cuba to keep her safe during Castro's regime"— Provided by publisher. • Identifiers: LCCN 2021017504 | ISBN 9781534469242 (hardcover) | ISBN 9781534469235 (paperback) | ISBN 9781534469259 (ebook) • Subjects: LCSH: Graphic novels. | CYAC: Graphic novels. | Stories without words. | Immigrants—Fiction. | Coming of age—Fiction. | Cubans—Brooklyn (New York, N.Y.)—Fiction. • Classification: LCC PZ7.7.C3748 Is 2022 | DDC 741.5/973—dc23 • LC record available at https://lccn.loc.gov/2021017504

Miguel y Zoraida
1944
El Tropicana
1945

La boda de ('48)
Miguel y Zoraida
Zoraida mirando la
Canastilla de Marisol

Habana, Cuba
1958
¡CLAC!
¡CLAC!

Calentico
MANÍ
PIÑAS
YCOCOS

Calentico
MANÍ
1

BODEGA
Siempre, quiéreme siempre
Tanto como yo a ti
Nunca, nunca me olvides
Dime, dime que si.
TOWN
COUNTRY
OFF
INT
INT LIGHTS
MAP
WIPERS

JARDÍN BOTÁNICO
SOLEDAD

¡ROMPER!

¡FUACATA!

9359

Amistad funesta
LORCA
OBRAS
Nuestra América
Bodas de sangre Yerma

LORCA

QUI QUI RI QUÍ

ESCUELA PRIMARIA
FRANCISCO BORJAS
DESDE 1937
Marisol

¡REVOLUCIÓN!
PATRIA O MUERTE
BATISTA HA PERDIDO A CUBA

ESTA ES TU CASA
FIDEL
Habana, Cuba
1961

LIBRERÍA DEL CENTRO

LIBRERÍA DEL CE

¡Besito!

BANG!
BANG
BANG
BANG
BANG

¡VENCE
PROYECTO D
ALFABE

¡APOYE LA ALFABETIZAC
6 de JULIO
ALFABE
HOMBRES Y MUJERES JÓVENES
¡UNANSE AL EJÉRCITO DE TRABAJADORES JÓVENES POR LA ALFABETIZACIÓN!
APOYE ★ LA ★ ALFABETIZ

9359
Szzz
Szzzz
GRRRR

¡BOOM!

¡WAHHH!

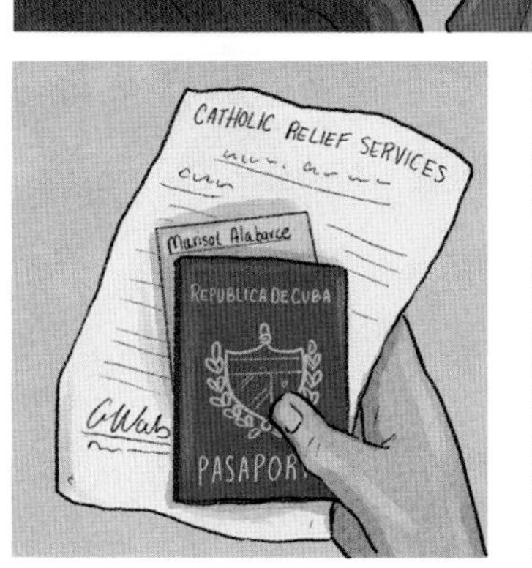
CATHOLIC RELIEF SERVICES
Marisol Alabarce
REPUBLICA DE CUBA
PASAPORT

9359

ZZZZZ

HABANA

Rancho-Boyeros Airport

¡PARAR!

Tú eres
Marisol.

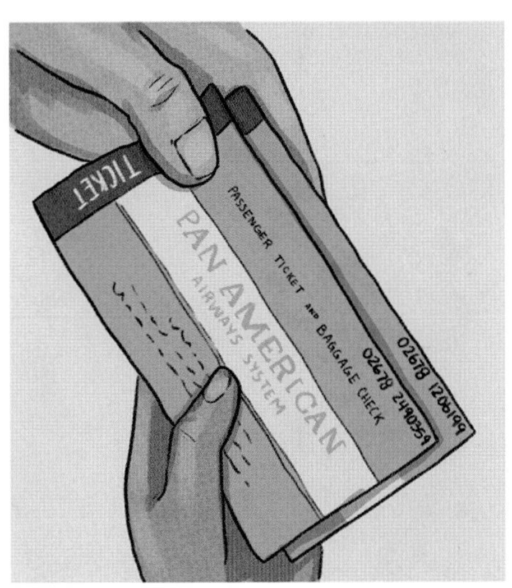

TICKET
PASSENGER TICKET AND BAGGAGE CHECK
PAN AMERICAN
AIRWAYS SYSTEM
02678 2490359
02678 1206199

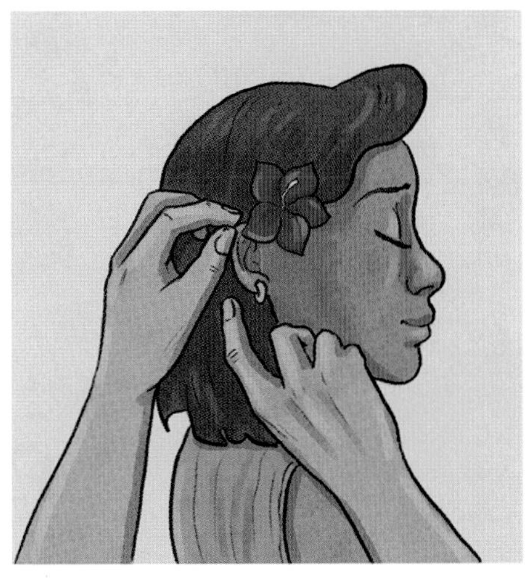

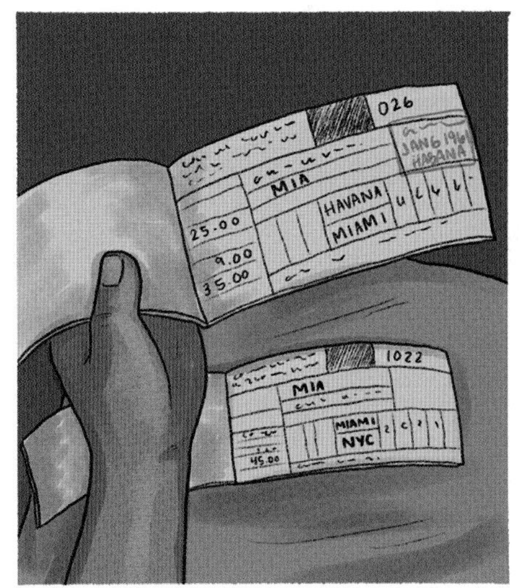
026
MIA
HAVANA
MIAMI
25.00
9.00
35.00
1022
MIA
MIAMI
NYC
45.00

Habana
Camp
Matecumbe
Miami

PAN AM
New York
City

NEW YORK INTERNATIONAL AIRPO
NYC TAXI
1022
PA

Welcome home Marisol!

FRESH BAKED
Is your heart . . .
. . . Filled with pain?
PLYMOUTH
Tell me dear . . .
. . . are you lonesome tonight?

Crr
Crrr

¡clic!

GIRO

¡TOK!
¡TOK!

¡BOSTEZO!

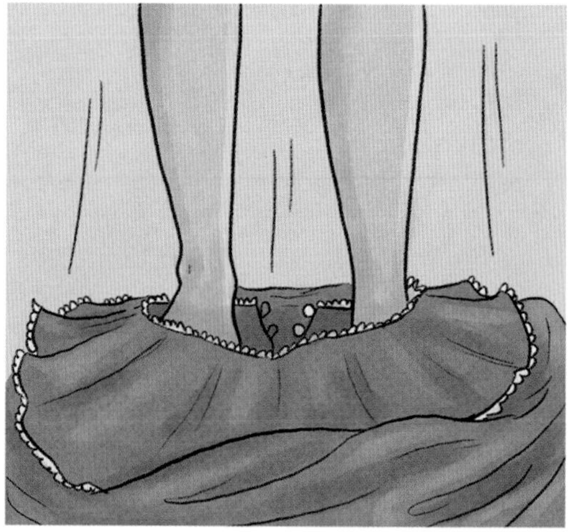

FSSSH
FSSSH

¡CRRK!

¡AH!

SHK
SHK
SHK

P.S. 48 WINTER FAIR!

¡FWOOSH!
Aa Bb Cc Dd Ee Ff Gg
Huckle
1. WHO
2. WHAT
¡FSH!
?
¡JA!
¡JA!

WINTER
SPRING
SUMMER
FALL
BE FRIENDLY
NOT RUDE

THE WORLD MAP
Aa Bb Cc Dd Ee Ff Gg Hh
Vocabulary
1. benefit
2. catastrophe
3. expression
4. reluctant
5. cope
6. dialogue
7. librarian
8. literature
9. undaunted
MS. JOHNSON

PRE-ALGEBRA
WORLD HISTORY
ENGLISH
SCIENCE
¡PAF!

PRE-ALGEBRA
WORLD HISTORY
ENGLISH VOL II
SCIENCE

¡ROZAR!

WORLD HISTORY
SCIENCE

B4
English Class

¡POM!

English Class
Suzie is baking a
noun
verb

Aa Bb Cc Dd Ee Ff Gg Hh Ii
F
Marisol Alabarce
INSTRUCTIONS
A B C
1 2 3 4 5
¡KRRR!
¡KR!

¡DING!
¡DING!
P.S. 48
WINTER
FAIR!
¡GOLPE!

JA
JA
JA
JA
JA
JA
JA
JA
JA
JA
JA
JA
JA
JA
JA
JA
JA
JA
JA
JA
JA

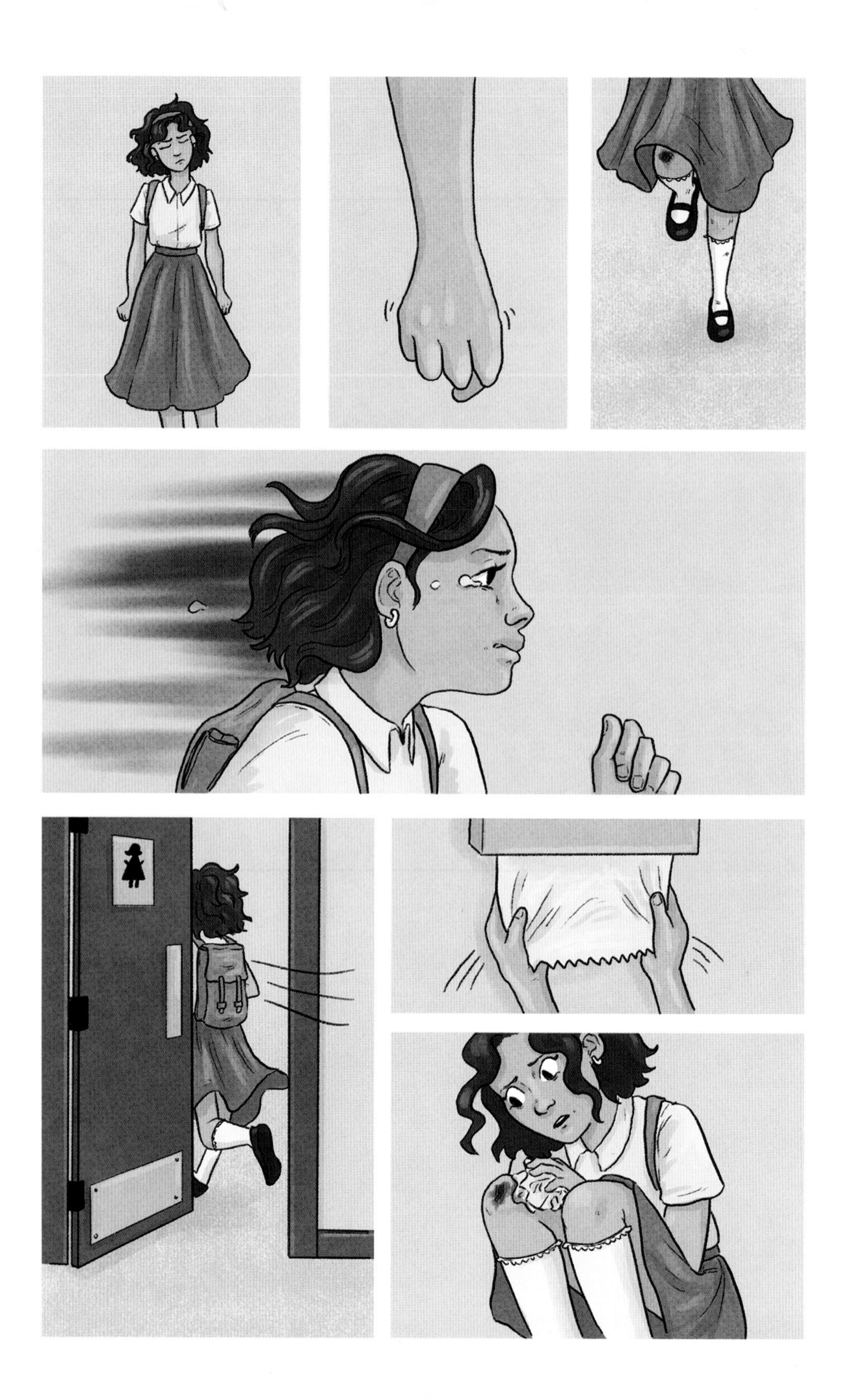

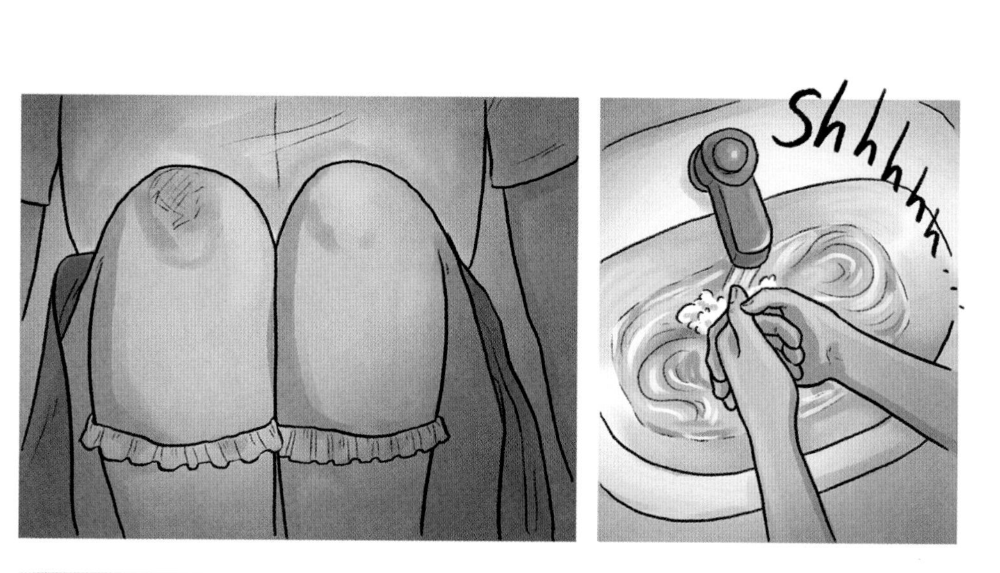
Shhhhh

P.S. 48
COMMUNITY BOARD
SIGN UP
P.S. 48
WINTER
FAIR!
FUNDRAISER!

ANNUAL FUNDRAISER!
FIRE

FIRE

Mami y Papi,
Hace mucho frío
y no me gusta !

CHRRRR
Mam
Te quiero.
Marisol

fft
fft
fft

Mr.+Mrs. Delfino
555 Carroll St.
Brooklyn, NY
11213
Paul Delfino
555 Sackett St.
Brooklyn, NY
11213
Jody Delfino
555 Sackett St.
Brooklyn, NY
11213
MR.+MRS DELFINO
555 Sackett St.
BROOKLYN, NY
11213

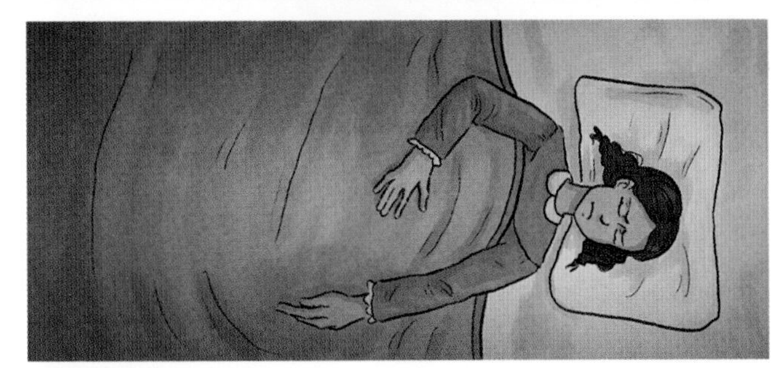

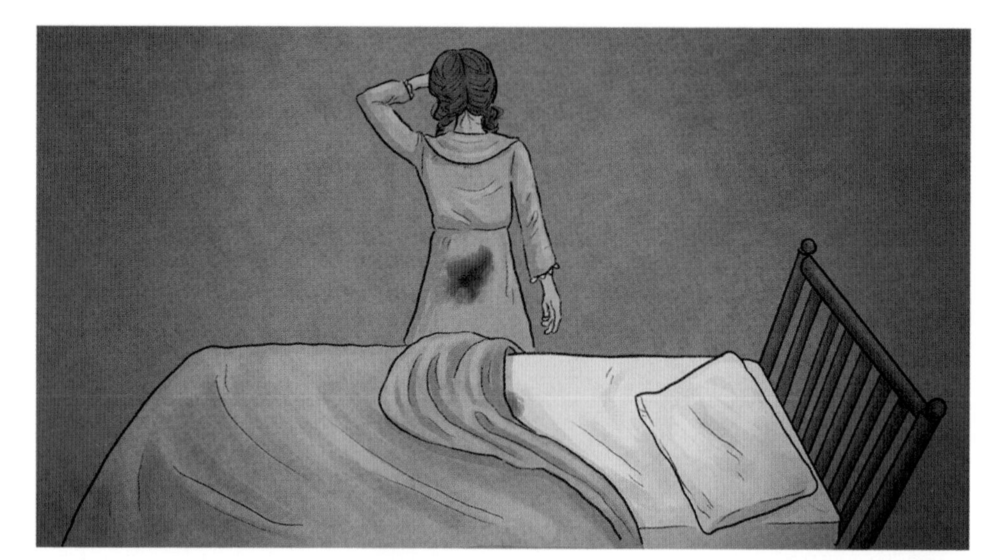

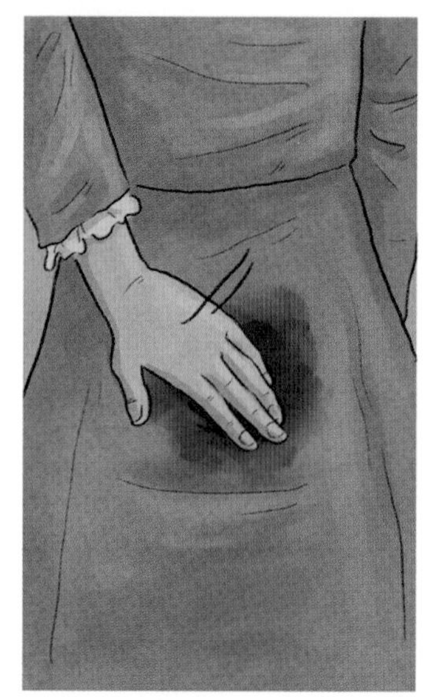

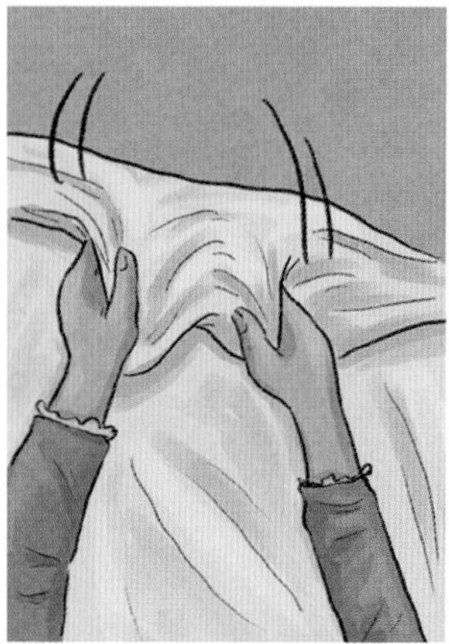

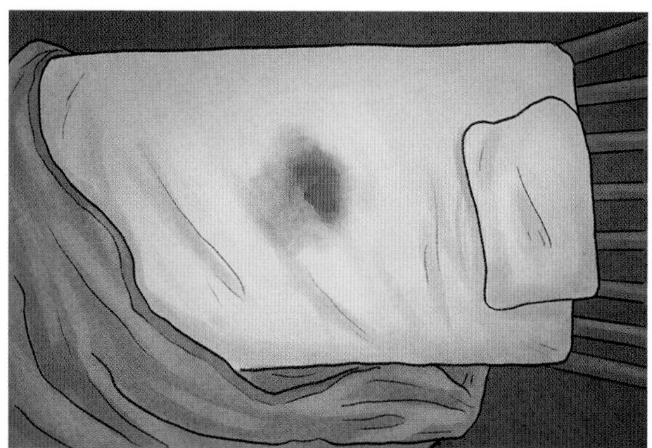

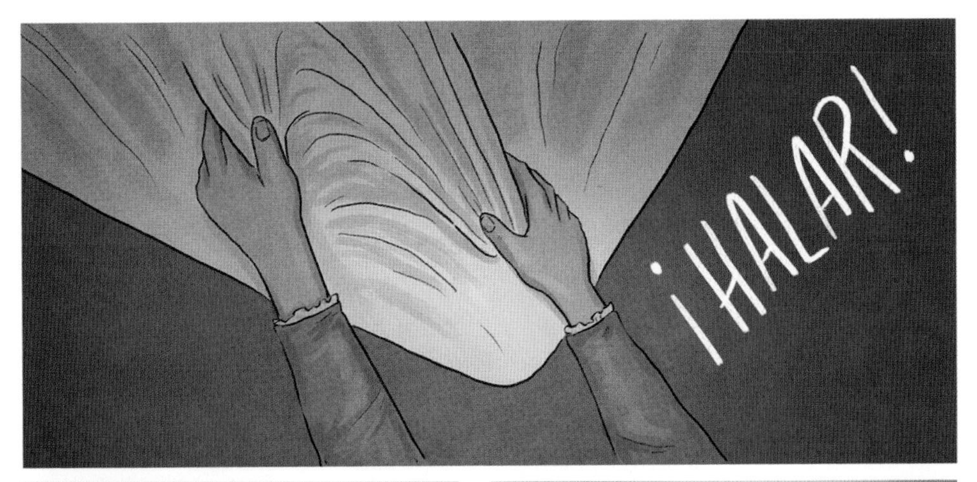
¡HALAR!

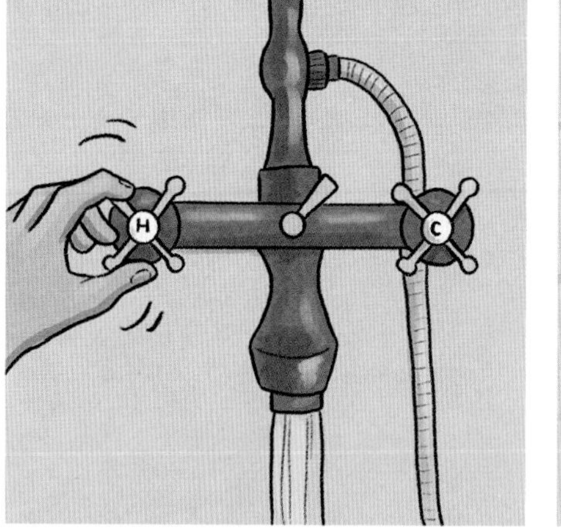
H
C

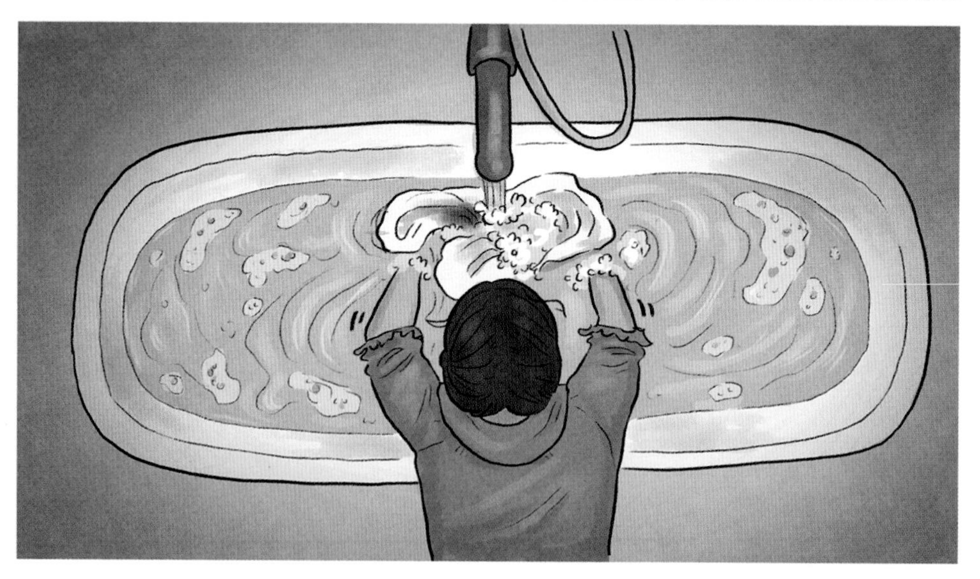

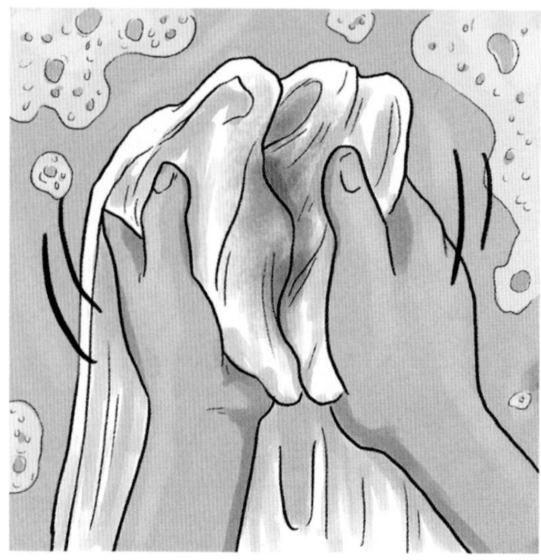

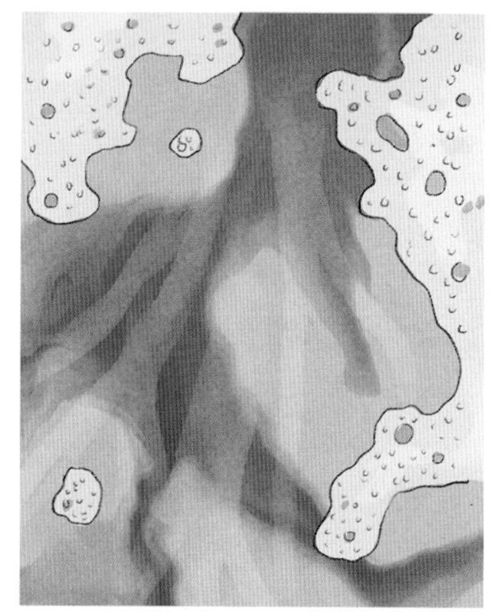

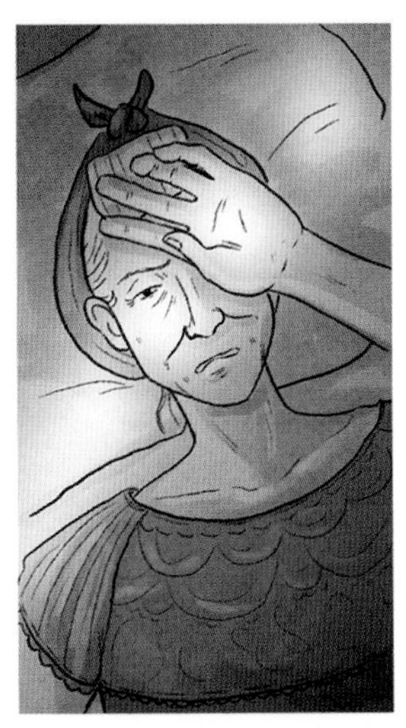

Tok
Tok
Tok
Tok
Tok

¡WAH!

KOTEX

?

KOTEX

KOTEX

KOTEX
TO BE USED WITH
1 BELT
12
12 NAPKI
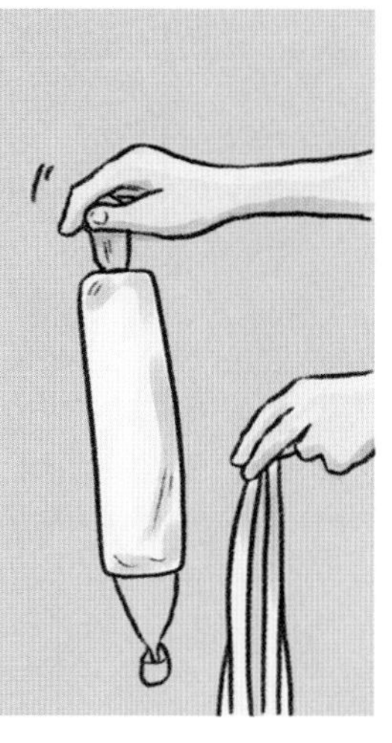

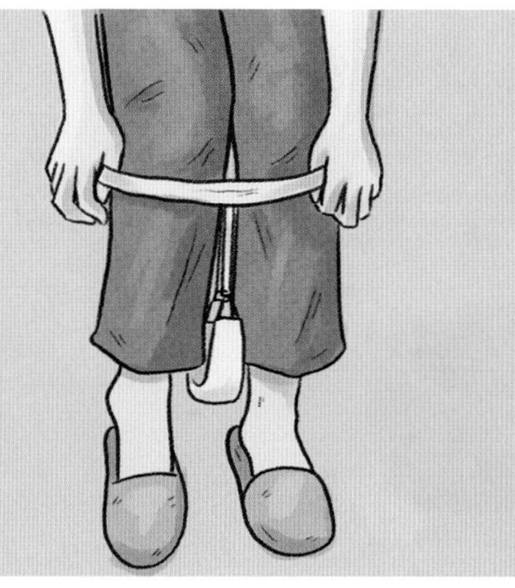

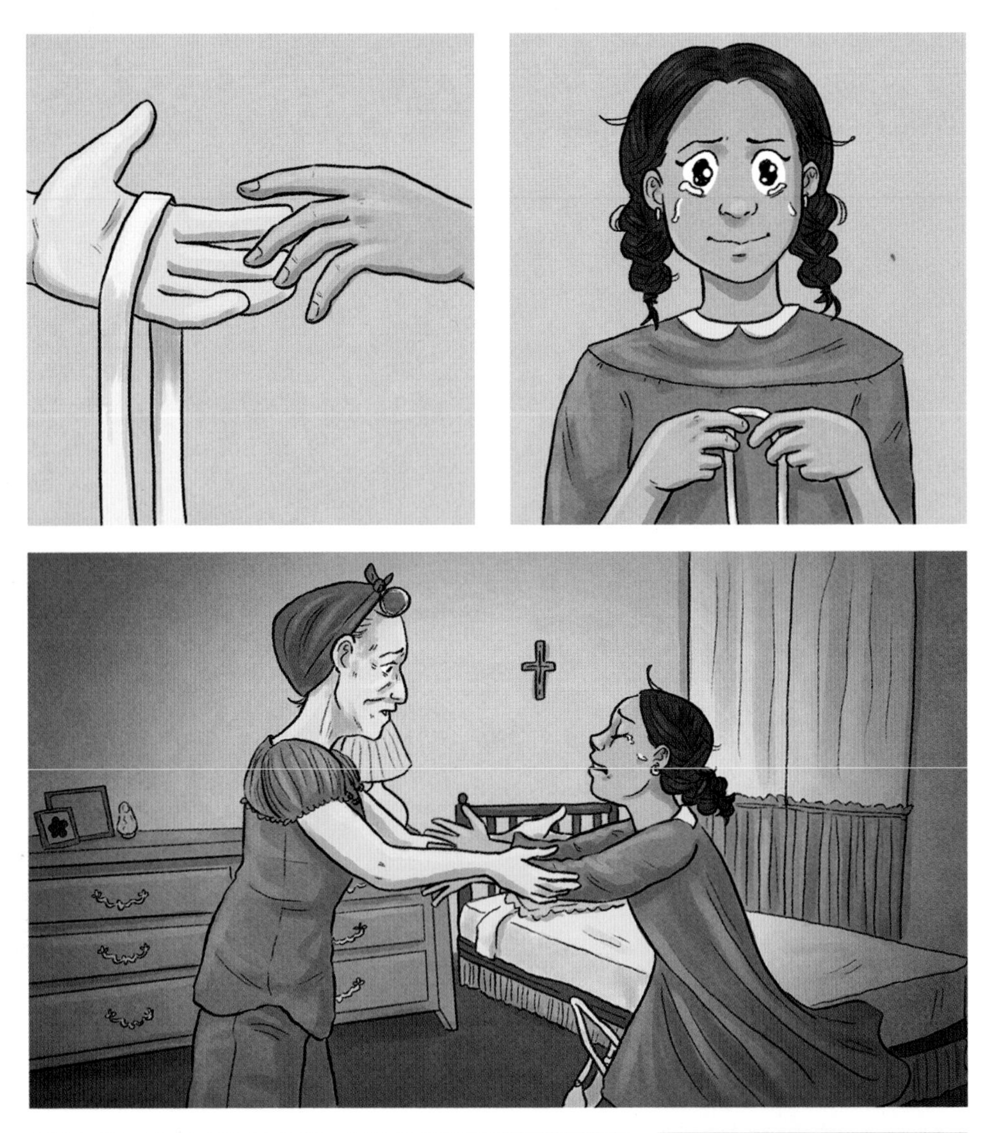

ANNUAL FUNDRAISER
FIRE

LIBRARY
RULES
RETURNS
TRASH
MARCH
Be-C

THE BOOK OF BIRDS
!

BURDIN PLANTS VOL I
NF Bu
BOTANICAL
NF CA
NF CA

Trees of New York
New York
York
Trees of New York
¡AH!
43
44
HAWTHORNE
MAGNOLIA

¡DING!
¡DING!
¡DING!

DROP

LIBRARIA

RETURNS
READ!

CRRSH

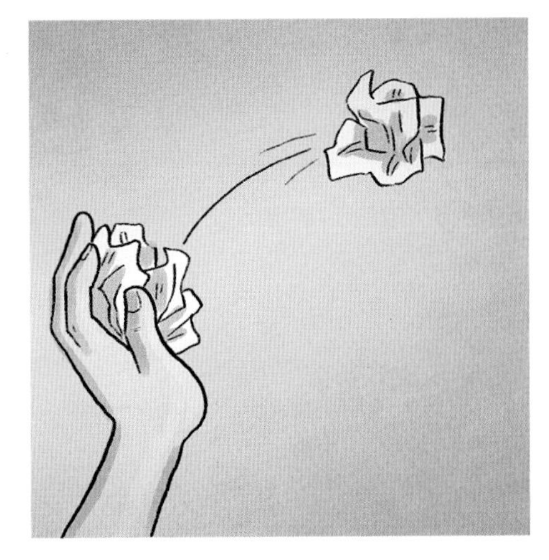

TREES OF NEW YORK

U.S. Helps Train an Anti-Castro Force
At Secret Guatemalan Base
NEW YORK
MEXICO
DIRECT
SERVICE
TWA

NEW YORK

Trees of
New York
Trees of
New York

Fig. B
Weeping Cherry
- 98 -
Fig. C
Crab Apple

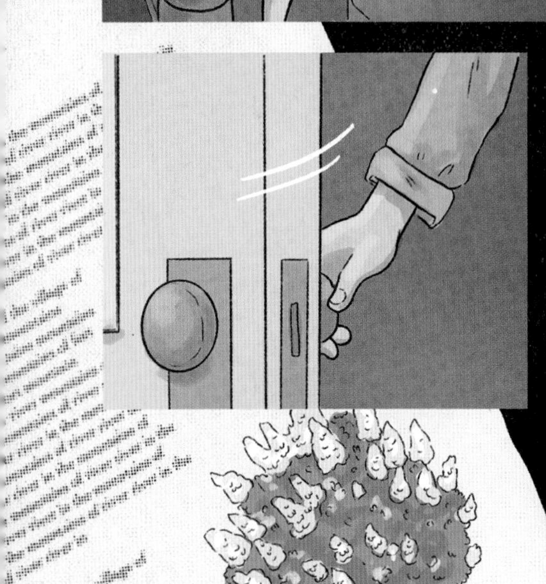

Fig. B
Crepe Myrtle
HAWTHORNE
Fig. A.
Hawthorn

Ginko
FIG 1
FIG 2
Crepe Myrtle
FIG 3
Crab Apple
Weeping Cherry
FIG 4
Hawthorne
FIG 5
FIG 6
Callery Pear
FIG 7
Saucer Magnolia
Kanzan Cherry
FIG 8

¡PANG!
Trees of New York

¡PANG!

¡PANG!
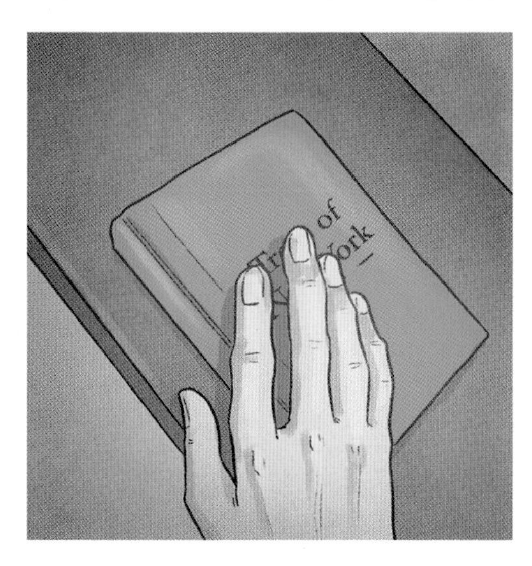

DELI
ROSSEN DELI
MEAT · PRODUCE · DAIRY
GROCERY
MEAT · PRODUCE · DAIRY
KULVIG DRUGS
PHARMACY

BROOKLYN
BOTANIC
GARDEN

¡PI-PIIP!

BROOKLYN BOTANIC GARDEN

GREENHOUSE

THE WHITE MARIPOSA
(hedychium coronarium)
Fun fact: Although not native to the country, the white mariposa is the national flower of Cuba.

GIFT SHOP

BIRDS OF BROOKLYN
BLOOMING TREES

ARIZONA DESERT
HOME GARDEN

ANIMALS OF THE NORTHEAST

AMEN.
Amen.
Amen,
Amen.
AMEN.
amen.
Amen.
B4
English Class
My na

Aa Bb Cc Dd Ee Ff Gg Hh Ii Jj Kk Ll Mm Nn Oo Pp Qq Rr Ss Tt Uu Vv Ww Xx Yy Zz

NOM
NOM
NOM
MILK

MILK

MMALS OF THE SEA
WHALES
MARINE LIFE:
VOL I
MARINE LIFE
VOL II
MARKS
FISH OF THE PACIFIC

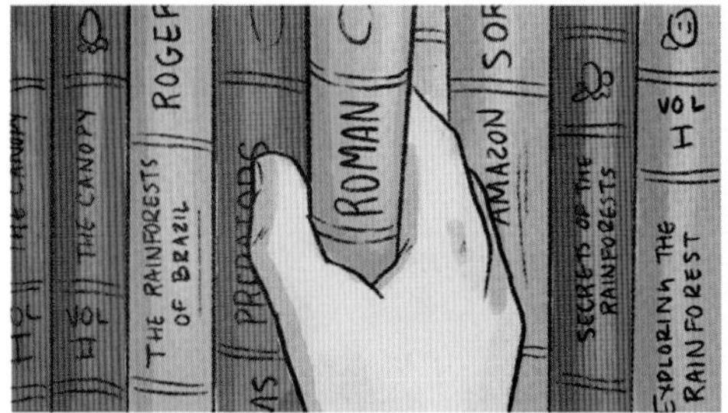
THE CANOPY
VOL
THE RAINFORESTS OF BRAZIL
ROGER
ROMAN
AMAZON
SECRETS OF THE RAINFORESTS
VOL I
EXPLORING THE RAINFOREST

TAP!
TAP!

LIBRARY CARD
Public School 46
Brooklyn, NY
Marisol Alabarce
Stamp!
FRANK NOBLE
APR
Maria Cane
SEP 359
Marisol Alabarce
MAR661

BRARIAN
SKSK
SKSK
BRARIAN
MATAHAMBRE DISHES
A Cuban Cookbook
BRARIAN
MATAHAMBRE DISHES
A Cuban Cookbook

PANG

HA!

Pollo
Arroz Con Pollo
(Chicken and Rice)

EZRA'S MARKET
EZRA'S MAR
GROCERY · DELI · PRODUCE
GROCERY
20% off Apples

ICKEN ROTH
ICKEN OTH
TOMATO PASTE
ROASTED RED PEPPER
PEAS
SHORT GRAIN RICE

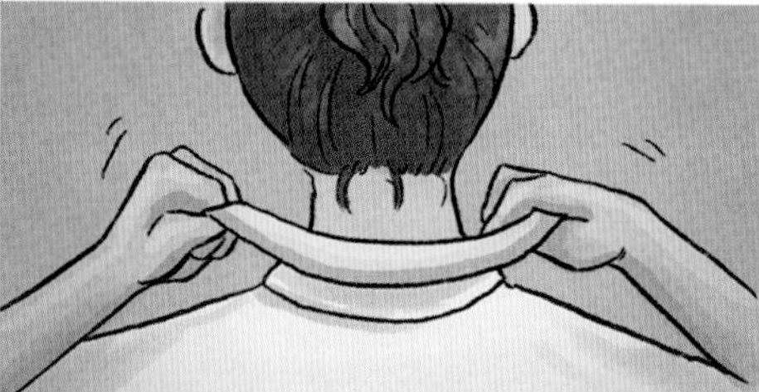

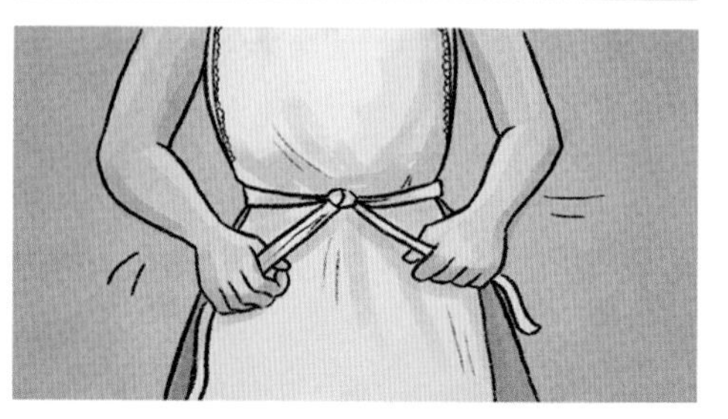

HA
HA
HA

TA TA TA TA

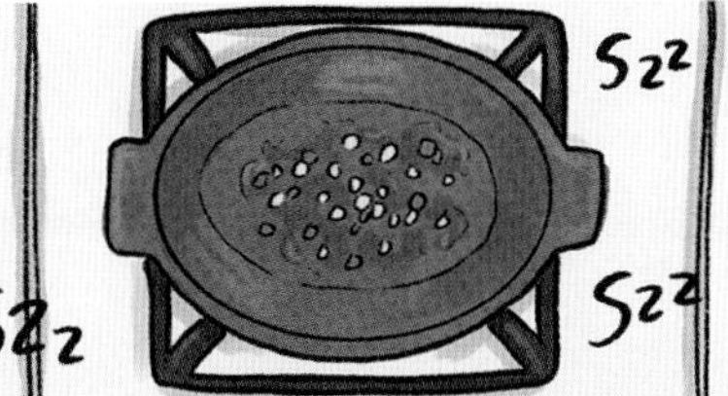
Szz
Szz
Szz

Szz
Szz

HA
HA
HA

CINDERELLA

Once upon a time there was a
gentleman who was married,
for his second wife, the
proudest and most haughty
woman that ever was seen.
She had two daughters of her
own, who were, indeed,
exactly like her in all things.
The gentleman also had a
young daughter, of rare
goodness and sweetnes
temper, which she took
her mother, who was the bes
creature in the world.

KNOK
KNOK
KNOK

TAK
TAK
TAK
TAK
TAK
TAK
TAK
TAK
TAK
TAK
TAK

TAK!

9359

BROOKLYN BOTANIC GARDEN
1961 BBG CHERRY BLOSSOM FESTIVAL
1961 BBG CHERRY BLOSSOM FESTIVAL

AIR MAIL
Marisol Alabarce
AIR MAIL
BROOKLYN
MAY5
1961
NEW YORK
Marisol Alabarce
555 Sackett St.
Brooklyn, NY 11213

KNOK!
KNOK!
SCIENCE

SCIENCE

Querida hija,
Te escribo estas cartas
mucho que te
Las cosas aquí no
todo que estás
sabemos cuando
juntos
Marisol Alabarce
555 Sackett St.
Brooklyn, NY 11213
BROOKLYN
MAY 5
1961
NEW YORK
AIR MAIL

Marisol Alabarce
555 Sackett St.
Brooklyn, NY 11213
BROOKLYN
MAY 5
1961
NEW YORK
AIR MAIL

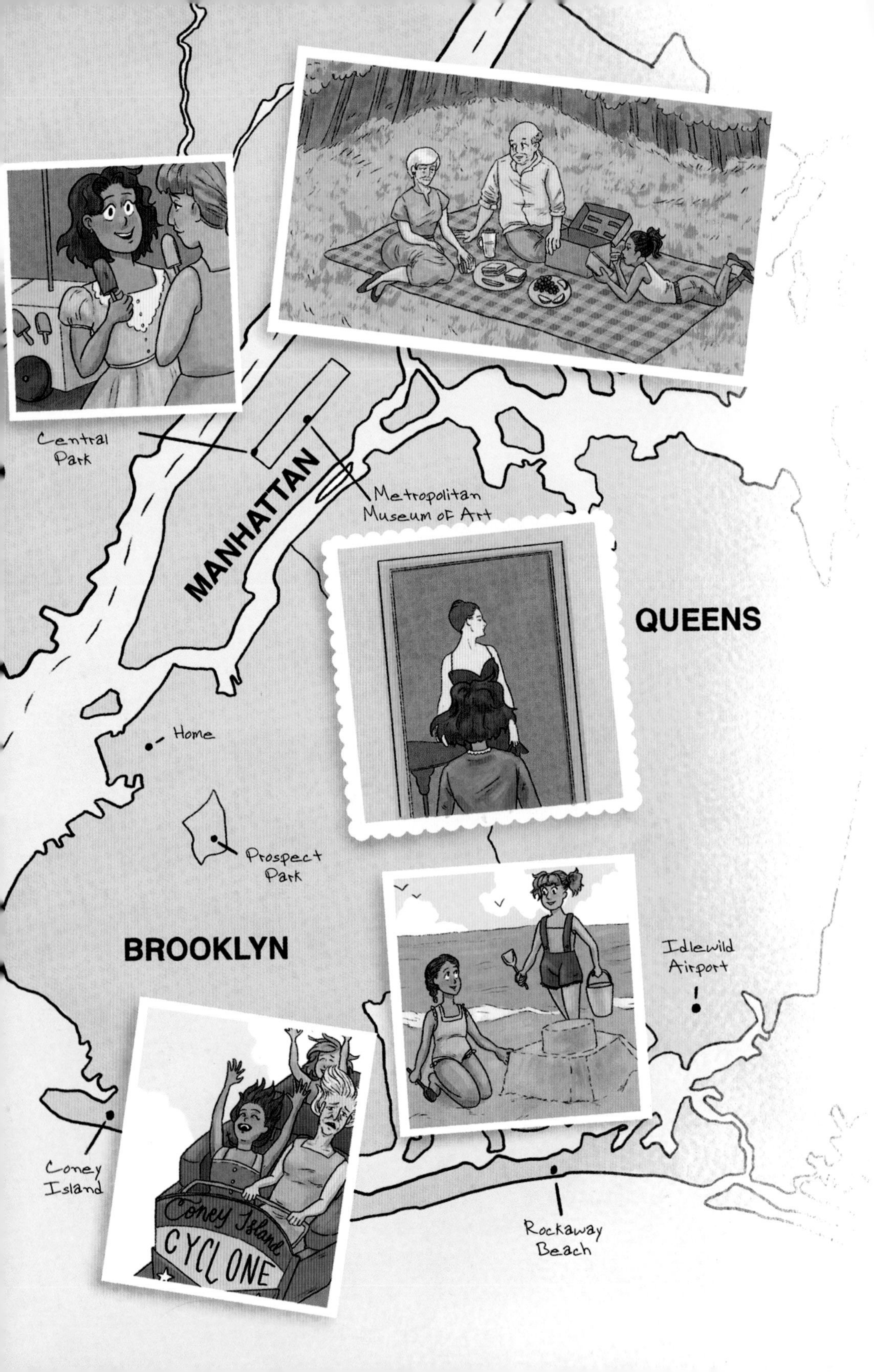
Central Park
MANHATTAN
Metropolitan Museum of Art
QUEENS
Home
Prospect Park
BROOKLYN
Idlewild Airport
Coney Island
Coney Island CYCLONE
Rockaway Beach

OLICHE

BENY MORE

Welcome Back!

Ms. Phillips
4C

Welcome to 7th Grade!
READ!
Library!

HA HA HA HA HA HA HA HA HA
HA!
HA!

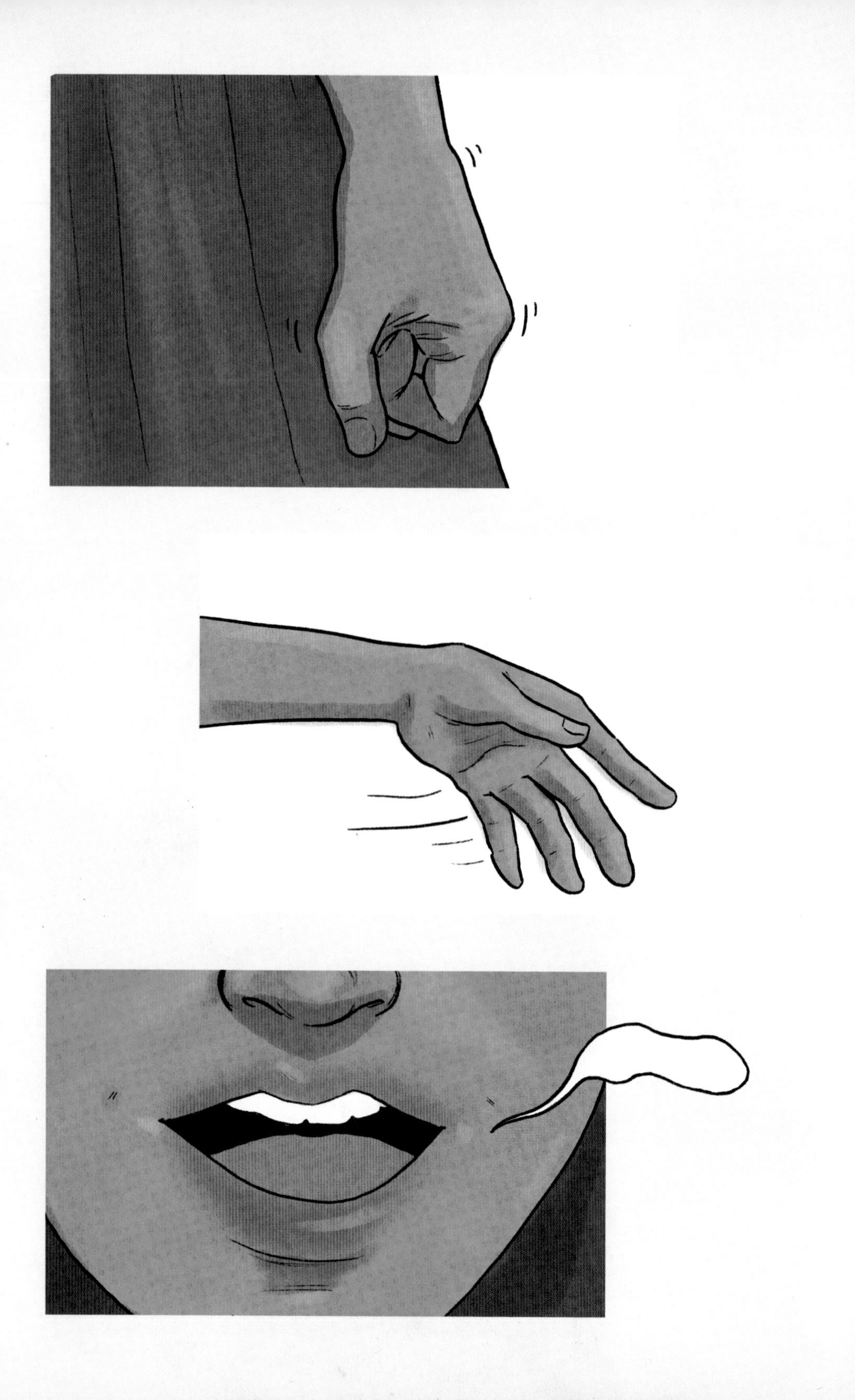

Hi, I'm Marisol.

('65) Llegando a los Estados Unidos

Los quinces de Mari ('66)

'67 High School Graduation

First day at work
1972

El bautismo '77
de Jessica

El 40 Aniversario de (’85)
Miguel y Zoraida

From Marisol's Kitchen

Arroz con Pollo a la Chorrera

For best results, cook with Cuban music playing and a trusted grown-up nearby.

1 lb chicken thighs	6 tbsps tomato paste
2 tbsps olive oil	6 cloves of garlic
1 green pepper	7 cups chicken broth
1 white onion	1½ tsps salt
2 cups short grain rice	2 tsps seasoning blend

Seasoning Blend:

1 tbsp corriander, 1 tbsp cumin, 1 tbsp garlic powder, 2 tsps oregano, 1 tsp black pepper, 1 tsp onion powder

1. Dice green pepper and onion. Thinly slice garlic. Wash rice. Season chicken with salt and pepper.

2. On medium-high heat in a large and shallow pan, brown both sides of the chicken thighs for 5 minutes.. Set aside.

3. Add olive oil, green pepper, and onion to pan. Once softened, add garlic. Cook for 30 seconds and add tomato paste. Stir and cook down the tomato paste for 1 minute. Add seasoning blend.

4. Add rice to pan and cook for 1 minute. Add chicken thighs back to pan.

5. Add broth to pan. Reduce to medium-low heat and let simmer, covered, for 1 hour. If it begins to dry out, add more liquid.

6. Dish is done when the rice is tender and most, but not all, of the liquid has been absorbed. Serve with canned peas and sliced roasted red peppers.

Enjoy!

Acknowledgments

I am lucky to have so many amazing people in my life who have contributed to bringing *Isla to Island* to life. Without their constant support, I would not have been able to make my dream come true.

First, I have to thank my mother, Maria Elena Castellanos, without whom this story would not exist. Thank you for taking me to the bookstore every weekend, for supporting every interest I ever had, and for making every sacrifice along the way so I could be happy. And to my dad, Frank Martinez, the best partner in crime a daughter can ask for. Thank you for being by my side all these years. I hope to be the copilot for you on many more trips, but you have to start being a better listener! I didn't say "snacks" that day!

And to Jorge A. Gonzalez *head nod of acknowledgment*.

To my brilliant agent, Marietta Zacker, who fell in love with Marisol and her story. I am so lucky to have found someone who wanted my book without words. There is no better cheerleader in my corner than you!

To my editor, Alex Borbolla, who made my dream come true. Thank you for understanding my book and for, above all, believing in me. And my designer, Karyn Lee, whose brilliant eye helped me whip this book into shape. With guidance from both of you, I've been able to produce something I am so very proud of.

To Jeannie Ng, Tatyana Rosalia, Milena Giunco, and the rest of the Atheneum team—thank you for all your hard work on this book!

To Reed Trachy—this book could not have been finished without you. Thank you for taking care of me when I was so busy with work, for taking care of my cat and being so dedicated to her poop watch, and for supporting me in all my impulsive endeavors. You make it possible for me to chase my dreams, and I will always be so grateful for that. I am so lucky to have you in my life.

To Sasha Glinski, who has been my creative partner in all things. Without your ambition and creativity beside mine, I would not have made it here. I still remember standing in the Crown Heights apartment bathroom, filled with anxiety and doubt about being able to do this book. Your words that night gave me the confidence to do this. Ashley Burdin, who knows the words in my mind before I can even form them in a comprehensible sentence—your insight and brilliance make me a better writer, and your friendship gets me into trouble—the good kind!

To Ali Hinchcliff and Hailey Rutledge, whose invaluable support has kept me afloat. I miss you both dearly and hope to celebrate many more Friendsgivings together. To Josh Rios and Jackie Smith, friends I can always call on, who will cheer me on and tell me to take it easy when I need to slow down.

And the Cult, whose friendship and insight has made the journey to becoming an author much easier. Meg Kohlmann, who helped me with my early manuscript and my query letter. Katy Rose Pool, Akshaya Raman, Tara Sim, and Melody Simpson, who welcomed me to the West coast. Janella Angeles, Erin Bay, Madeline Colis, Kat Cho, Mara Fitzgerald, Amanda Foody, Amanda Haas, Christine Lynn Herman, Axie Oh, and Claribel Ortega—thank you for welcoming me to the group and letting me cook at Culttreat. It's so wonderful to have you all by my side as we go on this journey together.

To the Art Hut, thank you for inviting me in and allowing me to grow and learn alongside all of you. You're all so talented, and I'm so lucky to call you my friends and be able to turn to you when that face looks weird, right? Something is off about this face . . . What is it? Your collective eyes have saved me over and over again.

And thank you to Isaac Durrington, Ryan Hansen, Lo Shdo, and Laudann Taravati. While working, I was dealing with horrible hand pain that I couldn't control. Without your help I would not have been able to finish this book. Thank you for sticking with me and trying your hardest to find solutions.

And thank you, reader, for picking up this story of a girl whose words couldn't reach you but whose story still could.

Operation Peter Pan

Cuba has had a rocky history since colonization. Several governments came and went, some better than others, and not all good. Cubans have fought over and over again for centuries for their freedom. Fulgencio Batista—the man Fidel Castro would later overthrow—was first elected president in 1940. He was supported by both the socialist and communist parties in Cuba, and his work did have positive results on the island. After his presidency he went to the United States, where he stayed until he decided to run for president again in 1952, but support for him had waned, and he lost. He followed this loss with a coup and removed the elected president, placing himself back in office. Batista's second presidency was nothing like the first. He was corrupt, allowing US interference in their country and allowing organized crime from the United States to settle into Havana. Batista grew more tyrannical as time went by and instated a secret police force that targeted those who opposed him, but especially those with communist and socialist ideals.

In 1959, a man named Fidel Castro and his rebels overthrew the Cuban government to became Cuba's prime minister. Not everyone agreed with Castro's politics or ideas, and he did not like people who disagreed with him. Many Cubans feared for their lives and worried that their children would be sent to prison camps as punishment for their political beliefs. They thought the best way to keep their children safe would be to send them away, if only until Castro's government fell. Cuba had already experienced several dramatic changes in government since they gained independence from Spain.

Operation Peter Pan was started by Father Bryan O. Walsh, who was the director of a Catholic charity in Miami, Florida. Father Walsh first learned of Cuban families' plight when people came to his charity for assistance after taking in young family members from Cuba. He realized many more kids would need help, and decided to do something about it. His program quickly gained support from the United States government—offering visa waivers and foster programs for the children—as well as from Cuban exiles, who donated to the cause, eager to help children avoid indoctrination from Castro's regime.

But all of this had to remain a secret from Castro and his supporters. In Cuba, a whisper network formed to spread news of this program so that families could apply to send their children to the United States, where they would be cared for until they could be reunited with their families. Even the American press agreed to keep these goings-on secret, allowing for the program to go undetected by Castro's regime.

Operation Peter Pan lasted two years (1960–1962), ending abruptly when the Bay of Pigs incident stopped all flights between the United States and Cuba. In the end, more than fourteen thousand children came to the United States from Cuba as exiles. It was the largest exodus of children of the twentieth century.

While the program potentially saved many lives, it was not perfect. Errors were not uncommon: sometimes children with family in the United States were not immediately placed with their relatives, or they were sent to group homes for juvenile delinquents instead of foster homes. Some children were placed with foster parents who became a second set of parents for them, but some were sent to homes where they were mistreated. It was a risk for families to send their kids alone to another country, but many believed it to be the best, if not the only, choice they had.

If you'd like to read a true account of a Peter Pan child, I recommend reading books from people sharing their personal accounts, some of which I have listed at the end of this book.

Author's Note

This book is a work of fiction inspired by my family's experiences, both in Cuba and in New York City. I wasn't raised on stories of mythical creatures or princesses in towers—I was raised on the stories of my family, their lives in Cuba, and, later, the lives they made for themselves in the United States. My picture books were the photo albums my family brought to the United States, one of the few precious items that made the journey.

I loved to hear these stories from my abuelos about the finca outside of Havana, and the pet dog, Saguita, who was taken on drives to get ice cream. It wasn't until I was older that my family shared the more difficult stories with me about the xenophobia and racism they faced, the true horrors of Castro's regime, and all the things we lost.

While some of my family were Pedro Pans (what children who went through Operation Peter Pan are called), my parents came to the United States a few years later through the Freedom Flights. Much of my mother's story inspired Marisol's.

My mother was younger than Marisol when she landed in the United States, and no one in her family could speak English very well. Her parents relied on her to translate things when even she could not speak the language much better than them. She was bullied relentlessly by the children at school and took it upon herself to learn English. Like Marisol, my mother was able to teach herself English by picking up books in the library.

I do want to acknowledge that Marisol's story is just one example of the immigrant experience, though. Immigration in the United States is a complicated subject, often tied closely to prejudice. If Marisol had a different skin color or religion or even if she was from a different Spanish-speaking country, her story would look very different—and most likely much, much harder. For example, five years before Operation Peter Pan took place, Eisenhower's government—the same government that would provide visa waivers for Cuban children—committed the largest mass deportation in American history. Nearly 1.3 million undocumented workers were swept up in the campaign to remove Mexicans from the United States. And, sadly, harmful anti-immigrant policies and rhetoric continue today.

Looking at today's unaccompanied minors at the border, the difference between their reception and Peter Pan's reception is night and day. There is no government-funded program to help these children; there is no promise they will be reunited with their families one day. Marisol and many real-life Cuban immigrants got a happy ending that is not guaranteed for others.

But what I hope people take away from Marisol's story is the bravery and resilience of immigrants from all backgrounds. They leave everything and, often, everyone they know and love behind to simply have a chance—a chance to give their family safety, security, opportunity, a future. They survive living in a country that does not love them, and despite that, they find corners of their lives to fill with joy.

Further Reading

- *Operation Pedro Pan: The Untold Exodus of 14,048 Cuban Children* by Yvonne M. Conde
- *The Children of Flight Pedro Pan (Stories of the States)* by Maria Armengol Acierno
- *Havana USA: Cuban Exiles and Cuban Americans in South Florida, 1959–1994* by María Cristina García
- *The Red Umbrella* by Christina Diaz Gonzalez
- *Waiting for Snow in Havana: Confessions of a Cuban Boyhood* by Carlos Eire
- *Fleeing Castro: Operation Pedro Pan and the Cuban Children's Program* by Victor Andres Triay